'1

The Explorers

3

3
14

2015

/ OCT 2014

First published in 2010
by Wayland

Text copyright © Cynthia Rider
Illustration copyright © Sandra Aguilar

Wayland
338 Euston Road
London NW1 3BH

Wayland Australia
Level 17/207 Kent Street
Sydney, NSW 2000

The rights of Cynthia Rider to be identified as the Author
and Sandra Aguilar to be identified as the Illustrator of this Work have
been asserted by them in accordance with the Copyright, Designs and
Patents Act, 1988.

Series Editor: Louise John
Cover design: Paul Cherrill
Design: D.R.ink
Consultant: Shirley Bickler

A CIP catalogue record for this book is available from the British Library.

ISBN 9780750261173

Printed in China

Wayland is a division of Hachette Children's Books,
an Hachette UK Company

www.hachette.co.uk

The Explorers

Written by Cynthia Rider
Illustrated by Sandra Aguilar

WAYLAND

"Let's explore," said Zac.

"Let's explore in the garden," said Molly.

Zac and Molly saw the water.

"It's the sea!" said Zac and
they went to look at it.

"Oh, no!" said Molly. "Look at the shark in the sea."

"Let's run!" said Zac.

"I can see a big egg,"
said Zac. "Let's go and
look at it."

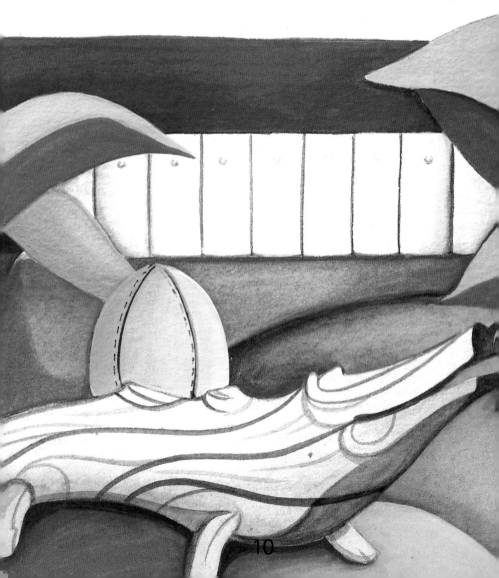

"Oh, no! It's a crocodile's egg!" said Molly.

"Let's run!" said Zac.

Molly and Zac saw a long tail.

They went to look at it.

"Let's run!" said Zac.
"It's a tiger's tail!"

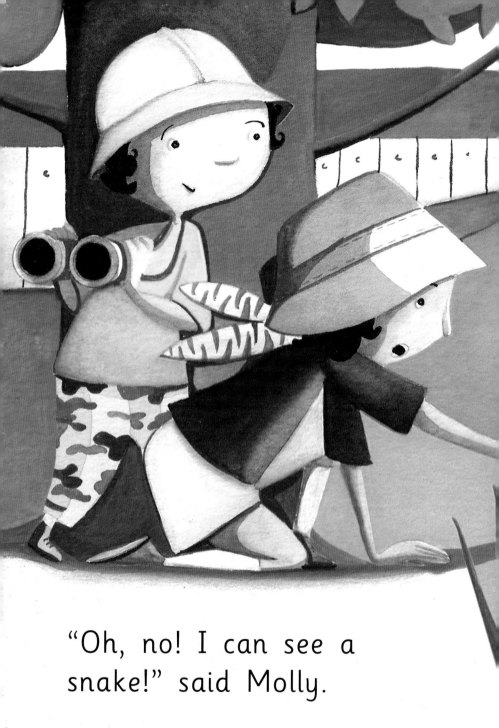

"Oh, no! I can see a snake!" said Molly.

"It's a big, long snake," said Zac. "It's a spitting snake!"

"Run! Run! Run!"

START READING is a series of highly enjoyable books for beginner readers. **The books have been carefully graded to match the Book Bands widely used in schools.** This enables readers to be sure they choose books that match their own reading ability.

Look out for the Band colour on the book in our Start Reading logo.

The Bands are:

Pink Band 1A & 1B

Red Band 2

Yellow Band 3

Blue Band 4

Green Band 5

Orange Band 6

Turquoise Band 7

Purple Band 8

Gold Band 9

START READING books can be read independently or shared with an adult. They promote the enjoyment of reading through satisfying stories supported by fun illustrations.

Cynthia Rider lives in the Peak District of Derbyshire and often finds inspiration for her stories in the countryside around her. She particularly enjoys writing for young children and encouraging their love of reading.

Sandra Aguilar enjoys the challenge of creating new characters and making them smile, shout or moan, which is why she decided to become an illustrator! If she had to draw herself her eyes would be huge and round and her smile would go from ear to ear.